Dr. Jeff Truzzel Benefactor of the World

I0665374

A tale of a man changing the world by pursuing his dreams.

By Hank Roberts

Published by Doctor's Dreams

PO Box 4808

Biloxi, MS 39535

www.Doctors-Dreams.com

writerpllevin@gmail.com

Prepared in the United States of America

ISBN: 978-1-942181-12-5

Dr. Jeff Truzzel Benefactor of the World

By Hank Roberts

Dedication

Dedicated to my special Wife of 55 years. We met in Jr. High, got engaged in high school and married the summer after high school. She has been with me, as my guide and inspiration, all through college and dental school. Janice has traveled with me to all of my mission trips and she is as familiar with all of the people we have met, as am I. Much thanks must be given to her for her organization of many of our trips. She was also instrumental in securing and packing the many supplies that we have taken to various areas. Without her assistance with clearing customs and managing our massive supplies, little could have been accomplished. Thank you from me and the many thousands of needy people that we have served.

Chapter 1

It was completely obvious why everyone who closely knew Jeffrey Truzzell believed him to be playing his life out with a few cards short of a full deck. To say that he was a couple of tokes over the line would be a gross understatement. The reason that everyone thought that Jeffrey was so odd was the fact that he was always making drawings and plans for some project that seemed, to everyone else, to be completely undoable and out of the realm of normal comprehension.

Jeff was a very likable young man. He just had a difficult time relating to other people, especially those of his own age. Perhaps he was just further advanced than most youngsters, both with his "way out" visions and his written proposals of projects, of which few could understand or grasp their meaning. He was raised in a normal household with a very average family. Although his parents did participate in many civic and social activities, they were not leaders who drove him to having his various ideas. His mother and father were both business people and were very serious about their work. As a matter of fact, they did not spend much time monitoring Jeffrey or his personal activities. They just lived the straight-laced life of normal, middle-class Americans. They had a nice, clean house in a nice neighborhood where nothing seemed to happen that was out of line or worth mentioning.

Jeffrey had many friends, some of whom lived a couple of blocks away and some that lived miles away. He kept in touch with them through his school, where all of the kids in his community attended. Often his friends would seek him out to assist with family dilemmas and also various school work and projects. Jeff was always willing to pitch in and assist a friend in need.

Although he had many friends, he was one of the people that was always chosen last on a sports team. He enjoyed playing sports, but he was not very good at them. He would often wish that there were not enough players to make up two complete teams. This meant that he would surely be chosen by one of the teams, even if it was their last choice.

Besides his friends, Jeff was well liked by his teachers and school administrators. He was very seldom late for class and he always had his lessons up to date. Grades were never a concern for him. Things seemed to just come naturally. Math, English, Science, Civics, they all were enjoyed by Jeff and he readily understood their concepts.

Once there was a fight after school. Two of his friends were having a heated disagreement. Jeffrey didn't want anything to do with this type of activity, so he stayed on the far side of the school. He had his bike ready to ride home when his friends returned from the fight. As most fights that occurred in the 1950s went, there was more yelling and calling of names than anything else. Maybe someone would end up with a black eye or a scuffed knee or elbow but that was about as violent as it got. The next day the principal of the school heard of the fight and called all of the children who had been at this brawl to her office. Jeff did not go to the office because he had remained on the other side of the school. The principal gave the boys a lecture and then she asked who had been at the fight but did not admit it and come to the office. All of the boys pointed out Jeff. He was then summonsed to the office. The principal said that she was very disappointed in him and his deception. Jeffrey tried to explain about his staying away from the area of the fight, but the principal wouldn't hear it. She gave him a paddling anyway and sent him back to class. The paddling didn't hurt as much as the disappointment that Jeff felt by having his friends betraying him, and also the principal not believing his side of the story.

From then on Jeffrey pretty much kept to himself. He would attend parties and outings with his friends, but he never again felt the same about them. He placed most of his attention on his studies, and his original plans for "way out" projects. He enjoyed making sketches and writing explanations of these projects. This seemed to make it easier for him to explain them to others, however they were seldom believed or taken seriously.

Chapter 2

In 1955, before the space age had begun, Jeffrey Truzzell found himself drawing and designing various rocket ships. He knew these ideas existed in science fiction, but also that they had not been developed yet. He was fascinated by occupying his spare time designing rockets. He would place the fuel tanks in place and make room for future space travelers. Jet engines were designed, along with sophisticated nozzle exhausts. The aircraft were taking on advanced designs and it was difficult for anyone in Jeff's classes to understand exactly what these plans meant. They decided to just consider Jeff to be a little strange and his designs, weird.

Often Jeffrey got in trouble in class because of his drawings. The teacher didn't want him to be wasting his time with "silly" projects, when he could be doing his schoolwork. Most of the time Jeff could show the teacher that he had completed his schoolwork and was using his spare time. The teachers would tell him to reserve these drawings and designs for his library time, when he could study what he pleased.

Although it seemed that no one was interested in his ideas or designs, Jeff continued to make sketches and diagrams of his ideas. His mind was filled with strange visions of futuristic development and he wanted to express them on paper. Jeffrey accumulated over 100 of his different drawings and detailed plans. He did not have the scientific ability or proper education to figure out the physics of the projection and launching of his rockets. He could not calculate the amount of thrust that was needed to send his proposed aircraft into space. He could not even predict the amount of fuel that would be needed for his aeronautic adventures. Jeff decided to just skip this section of his design and come back to it when he had the proper information. For now, he was satisfied with the design and drawing of his futuristic aircraft.

Once a teacher caught him drawing instead of working on the class subject. She took up his drawings and pinned them to the blackboard for everyone to see. Since rocket ships and spacecraft were not a thing of regular conversation Jeff was laughed at by the students and the teacher. It seemed that looking "outside the box" was not the regular way of thinking for his classmates. They could not see the future needing such things as rockets for space travel. Who would ever be able to project ourselves into space? Going to the moon was completely unheard of, let alone travel into deeper space. Information about other planets in our solar system, as well as other possible solar systems, was to be found only in detailed research books. No one knew if they were just speculations or if information about outer space was based on scientific facts. There was simply not enough knowledge about aerodynamics at the time for anyone who was associated with Jeff to understand. Their lack of understanding was what caused them to sneer at Jeffrey's ideas and designs. Jeff realized this and he took little heed in their disbelief. He just continued with his designs and drawings.

As his schooling advanced and Jeffrey became more knowledgeable about the things that he was designing, he began to expand his ideally designed drawings to other topics. He designed several "anti-gravity" devices, knowing that he didn't know the physics to calculate the actual usage of these ideas. He simply drew what he felt from within, with little regard for the rejection of those who viewed his drawings. By this time, the early 1960s, people were beginning to view scientific advancements in a new and brighter light. This eased the pressure that Jeff felt from his non-believing friends, but not completely. As time went on, Jeff's drawings and designs became more and more "weird" and unbelievable. His anti-gravity device design seemed to be little short of ridiculous. It consisted of an array of pyramids, arranged so that they might spin and create the anti-gravity force. The propulsion of these pyramids came from a nuclear-powered device that was located within the structure. After the device was started and operational, the continuing power was supplied by solar powered panels and some sort of storage batteries. The storage batteries were needed for the continuing power to the device when the sun was not providing direct energy.

A device such as this required many hours of contemplation and a number of sketches and designs. Jeffrey spent the better part of a year with his anti-gravity drafts and his adding and removing operational components that were changed along with the overall design. Again, no one took these designs seriously. Everyone knew that there was absolutely no way for the residents of earth to avoid the natural gravitational forces of our planet. After all, our planet was the product of a supreme being who must have meant for there to be gravity or he would not have created it. Red flowers were red and green leaves were green and there was no need to see things any other way than the way they have always been seen. It seemed very easy for most people to accept what they had been told and not bother about expanding their knowledge beyond what they had heard. It also seemed that the students, as they got older and higher in their grade standing, seemed to take on the beliefs of their teachers. No one seemed to care about being unique or thinking on their own. It was easier to just go along with the teachings of their classes because that would produce higher grades for them on their report cards.

I suppose that the final straw, for those who were considering whether Jeff was somewhat mentally scrambled in his thinking, was when he was assigned to make a speech in class on a subject that was completely estranged to his audience. He chose to speak on the solution of tensions between the governments of the USA and Cuba. This happened to be just before the Cuban missile crisis where Russia intervened. Jeffrey had 15 minutes to present his speech. He first outlined the basic plan and then he went into how he would enact that plan. Jeff's idea, in his speech, was to pump all of the dirt out from under the island of Cuba. He suggested leaving a little dirt, enough to hold the island up, and then telling the Cuban Government that if they didn't expel communism and install a new leader, the US would remove the remaining dirt and the island would sink. He explained, in detail, exactly how the US could dredge out the sand and mud from under the island. He suggested that the dredged material should be placed along the US shores and create a larger National fingerprint. Florida would receive the majority of the spill and they would create a larger state for recreational purposes.

Certainly this was a mythical plan and Jeffrey knew that it could never be accomplished. His classmates weren't sure. Before the day was out, Jeff's speech had circulated throughout the entire school. He became the laughing stock of the entire student body. No one knew whether to believe him or not. He had come up with some wacky ideas, according to their way of thinking. Jeffrey received a B+ on his speech. The teacher graded him on his originality, presentation, grammar, and his ability to hold the attention of his audience. He had stuck with all of these guidelines. Although the idea was completely "off base," he did get his point across in a very profound way – unfortunately, in a way that led to the complete dismissal by his friends and classmates of his believability and competence.

Later that year, one of the students who was running for student body president asked Mr. Truzzell to present a campaign speech to the entire student body. Jeff didn't know if the student really wanted him to speak about his election or if he just wanted to attract the attention of the audience. Attract the audience's attention Jeffrey did. As soon as he came onto stage to give his speech a complete hush came over the entire auditorium. It wasn't so much that the students were eager to hear what Jeff had to say but rather how absurd he would appear in presenting his message. Jeff began his talk by informing the students that there would be no student body president for the upcoming year. He paused and then stated that there would be no student body president if his candidate was not elected. After a brief hush from the crowd, they all broke out in a loud and boisterous laugh. They were completely entertained by what Jeff had to say. When the counting of the ballots was complete, Jeffrey's candidate won hands down. Perhaps it was difficult for people to comprehend and understand Jeff and his ideas, however his presence always made an impression. For the time being, Jeffrey would have to settle for notoriety rather than believability. He would continue with his futuristic plans knowing that no one would believe them. He could continue, however, knowing that he was recognized by everyone and they all knew that he had very lofty ideas.

Chapter 3

When Jeffrey went off to college the next year, he immediately began his studies of the sciences, the subject that he so dearly loved. He was a whiz at mathematics, physics, biology, and anything that dealt with scientific information and would provide him with backing evidence for his many fantasy ideas and projects.

Although chemistry was not his strong point, he did enjoy studying it. He was, however, a

complete failure in the lab. On two occasions his experiments exploded, causing a great deal of attention to be cast on the chemistry department by the school administrators. These explosions would not have been so notable, had Jeff been dealing with flammable or unstable chemical elements. He was, at the time of the explosions, simply working with basic chemical lab experiments. He did, however, tend to add additional chemicals to some of his experiments just to see what they would do. This addition of components wasn't quite so bad when he was doing physics lab experiments. They wouldn't blow up and cause a scene.

Jeffrey progressed on to advanced studies in the sciences. He even got a part time job teaching the lab section of biology. To his liking, he was only allowed to teach to the "non-science" majors such as home economics and all of the athletes. This was a great opportunity for him to rub noses with the football players and with the ladies of the home economics department. Several instructors complimented him on his ability to bring the grades up for most of these students. Jeffrey made it interesting for them by opening the lab at night and afternoons for special tutoring sessions. Whenever he was to give an exam, he would invite the students to come into the lab the night before the testing. He would explain anything that confused the students. He would even give the answers to most of the questions that would be on the test. Jeff wasn't trying to trick his students. He wanted them to know all there was to know about that subject. If he told them the answer and they remembered it, all the better for the students. He remembered how one of his physics instructors allowed his students to bring into class any reference material that they desired during their exams. The instructor was not interested in the students memorizing details. He was interested, however, in their knowing how to find the answers and solve the problems.

Jeffrey Truzzell, after having studied physics and mathematics on the college level, now found himself in quite a dilemma. He still got great satisfaction from dabbling with his original ideas and making drawings of them. He now, however, had enough knowledge about his futuristic ideas that he could put them into action. The question was, should he delve into an attempt to solve problems that were above and beyond the occurrences that were happening in his immediate experiences? Or, should he leave the larger projects to the physical engineers that were trained to handle these problems?

He had heard of nuclear reactors becoming overheated and the difficulties that arose from trying to dismantle them and rend them inert or nonfunctional. He was excited about making plans to solve the "runaway reactors" problems. Jeff realized that these reactors were producing massive power by creating enough energy to operate a large electric turbine. By producing their electrical energy, the turbines sent electrical power out to the various communities and installations that they served. This creation of electrical energy was very simple to understand. If you were to turn a turbine on the wheel of a bicycle, you could generate enough energy to power that device's lights. The real problem was in seeing and understanding how the nuclear reaction was producing enough energy to operate the turbines.

Jeff understood that there was an internal nuclear fusion going on within the reactor. He realized that the energy being produced was coming from this fusion. It was created by the removal of electrons from the outer shell of the atoms that were being used as fuel. The electrons were electrically charged and thus could be controlled by electrical impulses of an opposite charge. If one bombarded the runaway nuclear reaction with neutrons or protons, the entire reaction would be halted because of the lack of electrically charged atoms. It was just like removing oxygen from a fire. The fuel and the heat would not ignite if they were not exposed to the oxygen.

As Jeffrey proceeded with his plans to cancel the various runaway nuclear reactions, and thus make it safer for communities to use these reactors to produce their electricity, he showed the progress of his work to his instructors. The instructors, in turn, showed it to their superiors and the plans soon found their way to the United States Department of Defense.

One morning a knock was heard on Jeff's front door. When he opened the door, he was greeted by two Army generals and two full colonels. They were there to question him about his work with nuclear reactions. They explained to him that his discovery would be of great assistance to the DOD. After a lengthy discussion concerning his work and tying it to the use of the US military, Jeffrey was asked to disclose to the officers the exact schematics and plans for his idea. It was explained to Jeff that the military could use his plans to disarm any incoming missiles, or other war type devices, which contained a nuclear reactor. Remotely sent signals could also be used to bombard nuclear reaction war machines and rend them completely harmless. The military men told Jeff what a great military stride this would be for our nation, not to even mention peace in the entire world.

Jeffrey, or JT as he was known by his college classmates, was not a man of military knowledge, or even interest as far as that was concerned. He simply wanted to follow through with his several designs. He was not even interested in the monetary rewards that he might receive from sharing one of his projects, although this was stressed by the military men who visited him. JT told the officers that he would have to contemplate their proposals and give them an answer in the morning as to whether he would disclose his ideas and plans about this project. The men left with plans to return the next morning for Jeff's reply.

During the night, Jeff was awakened from a very troubling dream. He pictured the United States having his plans and all other countries having to bow to the wishes and demands of the US military. He realized that it would be extremely dangerous for any nation, or group of people, to possess his plans. They would be able to keep their nuclear arsenal and make all other nations' weapons obsolete. In his dream, JT visualized how the governmental officials, and military hierarchy of the US, as well as other nations, had misused and abused their positions of leadership. The welfare of the inhabitants of earth were not being considered, only the welfare of each individual nation. No longer would Jeffrey's idea and plans be used for the positive service of all nations. No longer would it be considered to control local nuclear reactors. Now it would be considered for military use to the degradation of all mankind.

Jeff had asked the military leaders to come back to his home at 10 a.m. the next morning. Jeff envisioned the dangers that he was now facing by exposing his ideas to anyone. He realized that many people had been "eliminated" for much less reason than he now possessed. At 9 a.m. the next morning Jeff was at the door of a local bank waiting for it to open. He had chosen a bank with which he had not had any previous dealings. When the bank doors opened for business, Jeffrey hurried to the manager and requested a safety deposit box, in which he placed all his current plans concerning the reactors. He locked the box and then made his way to the post office. There he sent the security box number, and key, to himself at his mother's home address. He called his mother and instructed her to securely hide the key when she received it. He also directed her to destroy the key if any harm should befall him concerning this matter.

Jeff returned home about fifteen minutes before the military delegation arrived. He politely advised them that he had decided to secure his documents and decided not to share them with anyone. JT was firmly and emphatically informed that he would be in serious trouble if he tried to share his project's information with anyone else, especially a foreign government. The men, aggravated by Jeff's answers, then left. They all got into a large black sedan and drove away. Jeffrey hoped that this was the last encounter he would have with these unfriendly and pushy men.

However, over the next several months, Jeff was approached on several occasions by the DOD, and also by private speculative investors, about working with them on his nuclear project. He always refused and told them that he had no intention of pursuing this project further. Never again did he attempt to open the safety deposit box, nor did he proceed with any plans that related to his work on nuclear reactions.

Chapter 4

Jeffrey had registered in the pre-medical curriculum when he first attended college. By the end of his third year in college he began receiving letters from different medical schools who were interested in having him attend there. JT's college had sent out letters of recommendation to several medical schools, based on his registering for pre-med., as well as for his outstanding grades. He visited all four of his top choices, Alabama, Tennessee, Georgia, and North Carolina. His major two concerns with the colleges were where he wanted to live and the quality and size of the school.

When visiting Alabama, he was impressed with everything but the gross pollution of the air quality in Birmingham. He felt like this was not where he would like to live. Georgia was a very nice, and adequately equipped school, but he felt that Atlanta was too large of a city for him. North Carolina was a little rough around the edges and it was also the longest distance from his home. This left Tennessee, which was located in

Memphis. It had fine facilities and instructors and met most of his criteria for attending.

When JT attended the pre-acceptance interview at Tennessee, he explained exactly why he had chosen them over the other schools. He told the interviewers that he realized that he had fine grades, he was capable of paying his own way through school, he was interested in research and discovering new medical procedures, and that he would be an asset to the college. He told them that he was not to be taken as arrogant, he was simply convinced that he and the Tennessee Medical School would be a great match. Rather than begging for admission, Jeff was simply pointing out his qualities and doing what he thought was necessary to gain acceptance.

The interview committee at Tennessee was very impressed with JT. Three days after his interview he received a letter of acceptance. Now he had his leg in the door with the big boys. They would have to break it to get him to quit now.

Tennessee, at the time, was on a quarter system. They attended school for 2½ months and took two weeks off. This allowed time for students to catch up on anything that they may have missed, and to spend extra time in gross anatomy classes or in clinical studies. This arrangement was ideal for Jeffrey because he knew that he would have good grades and he looked forward to the two-week break so he could spend time designing and sketching out some of his current outlandish ideas.

It was right after the first of the year when Jeff was to begin his official studies. For a couple of months before he started school, he spent his time securing housing and attending functions of the school. Each medical fraternity wanted to outdo the others by putting on the most lavish party. This was all new to him since he had not joined a fraternity in college. He was excited about seeing what this was all about. He stayed away from fraternities in college because he found that they seemed to all be based on how much alcohol one could drink and how many young ladies one could take advantage of. This was not his idea of a good time. He had heard that the medical fraternities were quite different and he was eager to see if it were true.

Jeff attended his first three parties at three different fraternity houses. Many of the students had housing there in the frat house but there was ample room for them to throw parties. The alcoholic drinks did flow, however it was not a drunken orgy or a party of ill repute. There was dancing and a live band. Some of the time was spent by the officials of the fraternity giving talks about their organization and the benefits of joining.

One of the things that JT learned was that there were about four large parties each year where all of the different fraternities and sororities of the different health professions at the UT medical center pitched in to defray the expenses. These large parties were held in different local facilities that could house at least 1,000 attendees. The fraternities also hired a big-name band to come and play. During Jeffrey's first two years at the school, they had Three Dog Night, Jefferson Airplane, Aretha Franklin, and

Credence Clearwater Revival, as well as several other well-known groups. At the time, these bands could be had for about $10,000. When all of the organization's money, along with ticket sales to the students, was taken up, it was easy to pay for these performers. The student tickets were only about $25.00 each. At the time, no one realized how famous these entertainers would become, but there were adequate ticket sales to support their performances.

Besides the large and small parties, the UT medical facility provided beautiful facilities for the students' use. There were indoor swimming pools, several basketball courts, a large lounge area where one could watch live UT football games, pool rooms, and much more. The officials of the school told the students that they wanted to provide the finest facilities, see that they had the best functions to make the students happy, and in turn they would work their butts off to become the best doctors possible. This excited JT. He concluded that he had chosen the ideal school for his formal medical training.

Jeffrey found housing in an inexpensive apartment complex that housed mostly health profession students. The UT medical center had schools for dentistry, nursing, pharmacy, physical therapy, and other health related studies. All of these schools were represented in the apartment complex. Although it was not in the best part of town, it was adequate and the price was right. $60.00 per month covered a two-bedroom, one bath, 700 sq. ft. apartment. Those who could not afford the rent secured assistance from different Church Denominations, who had offices set up for student assistance.

The only problem that JT found with his apartment was the area of town in which it was located. During Jeff's time in Memphis, Martin Luther King was assassinated. This caused much unrest among the local residents. Outside of his apartment, Jeff could see militants in the streets, burning houses and cars, along with total bedlam. One of the cars in Jeff's parking lot was set on fire and two bullets came through his front windows. Jeffrey called for help but the police were too tied up with problems around the city, so he crawled under his bed and went to sleep.

The next morning there was a man with a loudspeaker announcing that anyone who desired to leave to come out now and be escorted by the National Guard. Jeff wasted no time packing a few essentials and dashing to his car. He, along with several other apartment residents, followed the government escort out of the immediate area and to safety. His bad memories of that night caused him to never return to his old apartment. He hired a moving crew to go there and move all his belongings to an apartment on the far east side of town. The new apartment was farther from the school and it was more expensive, but Jeff thought that it would be worth it, not having to worry about his safety and wellbeing.

Because the new apartment was so far from school, JT bought a small motorcycle to make the daily transit. He found this to save him money on fuel, as well as help him drive on icy and snowy days. The people of Memphis were not accustomed to driving in the snow and ice and many of them would find themselves plowed into by another car or stranded in a ditch. Jeff could drive around the wrecks and carefully make his way in to school. Some of the students who rode large motorcycles teased JT because of his smaller bike. This made little difference since Jeffrey was not trying to impress them. His full concentration was directed to his studies. He wanted to become the best doctor that he could possibly be.

Chapter 5

Jeffrey studied hard and made very good grades in his basic sciences. The first two years were filled with the study of the functions of scientific theory and the understanding of human anatomy, chemistry, and pharmacology. There was little emphasis placed on business or administrative functioning. It was all directed to the actual medical aspect of being a doctor.

After Jeff entered his upper-class years, he found that there were many fields of medicine which he needed to consider. Every student was obligated to study and know all the areas of medicine, but most began to drift toward the medical field of their liking, such as emergency medicine, obstetrics, radiology, and the sort. At this point in his education, JT was centered on learning the basics of practicing his chosen profession. He figured that he'd have plenty of time to decide on a special field of study later.

Even while in medical school, Jeffrey kept making drawings of many of his "out of the box" ideas. He now had more exposure to different concepts, upon which he could base his ideas and designs. Many of his new drawings were targeted at medical topics and procedures. One of his favorites was having a patient ingest a nucleotide, or a nuclear charged medicine. After a short time, the patient could be placed under a full body x-ray scan and those areas of abnormal cellular development, such as cancer, would show up as bright spots where the nuclear medicine had concentrated. This would make it much easier for physicians to localize exactly where a problem area was located in one's body.

JT showed sketches of this idea to several of his instructors. They all showed quite a bit of interest in this proposal, however, they all tended to refer him to a particular medical research department. They told him that, after the researchers perfected the practice, it could be put into effect by the practicing physicians. This was just another step in the long path to a successful idea.

Jeff found out quickly that money and profit were the major driving forces in promoting most anything, especially pertaining to medicine. Very few ideas, and even fewer medical personnel, would find success in the field if they did not promise great financial rewards.

Many classmates were befriended by Jeffrey. He seemed to relate to most all of them. He did, however, have his favorites. One of his favorite classmates was a young man by the name Nick West. Nick was a studious type who took all his studies very seriously. He had chosen Tennessee to attend medical school in order to get a distance between himself and his father. His father was a very demanding physician who was the dean of a medical school in the North East. He had assured Nick a position at the school where he was dean, if only Nick would promise to live at home and continue to be "under his father's thumb" of constant control. Nick not only rejected this idea, he also went out on his own and secured his own acceptance to a medical school in the South East. Here is where Nick and Jeff met and became the best of friends.

All of the deans and staff of the Tennessee medical school knew of Nick's relationship to his dean father. For this reason, Nick obtained a special amount of respect from his instructors and the school's administration. Nick was very familiar with JT's eccentric ideas and had, on many occasions, been shown the several drawings and plans for these ideas. He never made fun of Jeff's ideas and often he found them to be quite interesting.

During one term at school, when Nick and Jeffrey were assigned to study and work together in the obstetrics department of the hospital, a very unique and life-threatening situation arose for one of the patients, with whom they were charged. After several medical tests were performed on the patient, it was found that the child within her womb was not developing properly. The first problem was that the fetus had an extremely deformed left arm. This deformed part of its body was severely draining the natural growth of the rest of the developing fetus. In addition, the unborn child had the umbilical cord wrapped around its neck and was having blood flow blocked from ascending to its head. Neither the students nor the instructors had a good solution for approaching a resolution of this problem. The only thing that they all knew was that the developing fetus only had about two days to live if something drastic wasn't done.

Jeffrey secured the attention of Nick. Both students went to JT's apartment where Jeff retrieved several drawings from a box stored under his bed. Jeff explained to Nick that he knew that it was farfetched, but he had made intricate designs and plans for the exact problem that was occurring with their patient. He showed Nick his plans of doing a cesarean section on the patient, partially removing the fetus, removing the deformed arm and suturing the wound, unwrapping the umbilical cord from around the fetus's neck, and then gently replacing the unborn child back into the uterus for the completion of its development. At this time in medical science development, this procedure was completely unheard of. Workable or not, this seemed to be the only possible solution.

Nick approached his instructors and proposed JT's written plans. When it was originally rejected, Nick pressed to know what other solution the instructors had. He pointed out that once a president of the United States had died because he required a tracheotomy, but since no one had previously done one, no one was willing to risk it. A physician present with the president suggested the tracheotomy, but no other physician would agree to it. It was simply too dangerous to cut open one's windpipe. The president subsequently died. Later this procedure became standard training for trauma surgeons.

The instructors agreed to the procedure suggested by Nick and Jeff, only on the condition that both Nick and Jeffrey would be present at the surgery.

The next day the surgical procedure was performed. Hands shook and breaths were held. Prayers were offered to assure the successful completion of this procedure. After four hours in the operating room, the surgeons appeared to the family. They all had smiles and reported that the surgery went well. The family was informed that the true measure of the success of this procedure would be how the patient did during the next weeks of her pregnancy. It was known to everyone that this type of operation would have to undergo much scrutiny before it would be accepted as a normal procedure. The family was informed that this was the first surgery of its type performed in the world. They were told that it was able to be done thanks to the foresight of one of their brightest students. The surgical details, along with Jeffrey's laid out plans, led to the beginning of a new procedure for obstetric treatment.

Despite the success, very little was said to the media about Jeff's idea and detailed plans.

This was perfectly all right with JT for he had not done any of his planning to gain recognition for himself. The recognition basically went to the several surgeons that performed the obstetric procedure. Jeff was more than happy to receive the admiration and respect from his instructors and classmates, which he well deserved.

While still studying in the obstetrics department, Jeff observed another problem that he felt he could possibly solve. Many children who were born of parents with specifically different blood types were born with erythroblastosis fetalis, a condition resulting in a "blue baby." The child was born without enough red blood cells to transport the oxygen needed. These babies required immediately blood transfusions to survive. Jeffrey created a plan to transfuse the blood into the fetus blood while it was still inside of the mother's womb. When he presented this idea to his instructors, they were not so quick to reject his suggestion. Because Tennessee was a major research hospital and it possessed many different facilities for testing various medical procedures, the instructors agreed to undertake the enactment of Jeff's idea. The idea consisted of determining the exact position of the fetus, stabilizing that position, and inserting a long needle through the mother's abdomen, through the uterus, and into the unborn child's abdomen. Specific desirable blood was then injected into the fetus. The new blood was accepted and the child continued to develop with the proper blood type. After the successful completion of the original trial, this procedure also became a regular in the medical treatment books of accepted procedures.

Jeffrey now approached his final months of formal medical school. He realized that Nick would soon be going his own way, along with many of his close friends and fellow doctors. Jeff had enjoyed serving the medical needs of others, especially the underprivileged. In Memphis there were several hospitals dedicated especially to the treatment of "less fortunate" patients who could not pay for their medical treatment. This provided Jeff with extensive experience in many fields of medicine. He was now faced with the decision of how he would plan to spend the rest of his life, with special consideration on his newly acquired medical skills.

Chapter 6

Dr. Truzzell was now a fully-fledged physician. He initially went into practice with another doctor, who was eager to have a young associate to cover some of his medical load. This was very exciting and Dr. Jeffrey soon had a very busy practice. It wasn't long before he had secured his own patients and he developed the wanderlust of going out on his own and being his own boss and business director. After two years of associated practice with the other doctor, Jeff decided to take the big step and go out on his own. This decision caused quite a bit of anxiety. Would his present patients follow him? Would he be able to make enough to support a new building and new equipment, and all his new staff? Could he take the despair of falling on his face after he had worked so very hard to get to where he was? So many questions and only one suitable answer. Jeffrey would have to venture out on his own or he would never realize what it really felt like to be an independent practicing physician.

Dr. Jeff had never been faced with dealing with finances on a large scale. He figured that he could do it, especially with his experience of working with outlandish ideas and futuristic plans. Off he went. First, he purchased some land that was very accessible to many local patients. Second, he secured an architect that would design him a uniquely styled office building. He wanted one that would stand out in the community but also fit in with the local architectural designs. Our good doctor found that hiring a good architect was a great idea. The architect oversaw the entire building procedure and Jeff simply had to sit back and watch as the building developed into a beautiful community structure.

All the local medical suppliers, along with the local hospitals, were constantly pestering him to give them his business. The pressure was on to choose the office supplies, medical supplies, and arrangement of the logistics of running an office. Once Dr. Jeff chose a supplier, he sat back and allowed them to supply all his medical office needs.

Everything went as planned. In four short months, Jeff was in his new facility and the office was running smoothly. All the locals had heard of his new unique office and he was flooded with new patients. He was also dealing with the patients that followed him over from his previous office. Long, hard hours were spent for the first six months trying to get everything organized so that the office would operate smoothly. One of the most difficult things for him to deal with was how he would efficiently deal with medical records and the filing of insurance forms. This all came together after things settled down and the practice smoothed out.

After about two years of practicing medicine in his new office, Dr. Jeffrey still felt a feeling of emptiness. He was properly treating all his patients, but he was not extending his medical knowledge to others around the world who also needed medical attention. When Jeff joined the local Rotary Club he found that they had several avenues of service. One of these avenues was international service. Rotary International had funds that were set aside for medical projects in developing countries. This was exactly what Jeffrey was searching for.

Dr. Truzzell volunteered to go to one of the islands in the Caribbean, meet with their Rotarians, and make plans for serving the needs of this underprivileged nation. When Jeff met with the local Rotarians of the Island, he was overcome by their huge needs. There was no air conditioning in any of the hospital clinics. Often five children occupied one hospital bed for there was not enough room for everyone. The ladies who had come to the facility for the delivery of their babies were placed two to a bed, head to foot. The laundry of the clinic was done by hand and placed over shrubbery for drying. These islanders were years behind modern technology and medical procedures.

Dr. Jeff was asked to look in on a patient that had been brought in from a car wreck a few days before. She was unconscious and laying completely nude and uncovered on a gurney type bunk bed. Her eyes were rolled back in her head and she had several wounds that had not been properly cared for. Jeffrey discovered a fly coming out of her mouth. He asked for a flashlight, which was the only source of intensified light that they had. Jeffrey discovered that the woman's throat was completely infested with maggots. They were obstructing her airway and the woman was dying from affixation. Dr. JT set up a makeshift suction device, of which they had none, and he cleaned out the patient's mouth and airway. It was all that he could do to keep from gagging at this sight, but he realized that this type of occurrence was what he was down here for. After clearing her airways, he began properly dressing her open wounds. He placed her on extensive antibiotics and gave her nurse instructions as to her future care. Jeff had brought with him a supply of different antibiotics and analgesics. Jeff realized that the patient was alive and would recover, due to his medical knowledge and service.

Located behind the clinic, and almost out of sight, was a small wooden building. It was about twelve feet on each side and had a small door in the front. There were no windows. Upon asking about this building, Jeff found that it was the hospital's morgue. Dead bodies would be taken out there and thoroughly iced down. Once a week a truck would come by and pick up any bodies present. Although this seemed archaic, it was very functional. Many of their medical facilities and procedures were just like that. They were rudimentary but served their purposes.

Although the medical treatment the patients received were necessary, their facilities were far from clean and acceptable. Patients had to bring their own pillows and sheets, if they were to have them at all. At one clinic Dr. Jeff inspected, the plumbing in the restrooms leaked and those patients who could walk had to make their way through standing water and filth. The meals were prepared for the patients on an outside woodburning fireplace. There was no running water in the kitchen for washing dishes or utensils. These, and all his findings, were targeted by Jeffrey as items that needed to be addressed. He made comprehensive notes of the areas that needed attention and kept them for reporting to the Rotary Clubs, which would help solve these problems.

On several occasions when Dr. JT was traveling to the islands to deliver a mobile health clinic, he would fill the clinic with supplies and equipment needed for their medical facilities. When the customs officer questioned why Jeff brought stoves, he explained that he needed to boil water and use heat to sterilize his instruments. He didn't add that he was bringing them to allow the cooking of hospital meals to be done inside and not on campfires. Three times he brought refrigerators in the mobile units. He explained to the customs officer that he needed to keep much of his medications refrigerated. These appliances were also needed in the hospitals so that they could store foods that needed refrigeration, such as milk, eggs and meats, without having to go to the market on a daily basis.

Dr. Jeffrey, through his many connections with high ranking government officials, arranged for the large mobile medical units to be delivered to the islands via military transports. One was delivered by a Navy ship that was making a layover there in Jamaica. One was flown down by a C-130 military airplane. It was a hurricane hunter aircraft and it was headed to pick up some hurricane equipment that had been left in one of the Islands. Another one, because of its size, was delivered in a C-5A, which was the largest transport airplane that the US government had. It served Jeff's purpose perfectly. So very many of these arrangements were made in coordination with Rotary International, that seemed to have some governmental pull.

During one of Dr. JT's visits to the islands, he was asked to go with the local Rotarians to a facility that the Rotary Club supported. This facility was a make shift school for the mentally handicapped. Upon entering the school, Jeff paused to look around the facility. As soon as he walked in, something came down on his head that almost knocked him unconscious. When he gained his composure, Jeffrey found that a large piece of roofing tile had fallen onto his head. The school director told Jeff that this happened several times a week. On a few occasions, the tile had hit one of the students. This was the best facility that they had available at the time of construction, and they couldn't afford to do repairs or rebuild. Jeff shook his head in total disbelief. He asked the Rotarians about this dangerous situation and they told him that this was the only place for the handicapped children to meet. Upon receiving this answer, Jeff immediately proceeded with the local Rotarians to find a piece of property that they could buy so that they could build a new and safer complex. This was quickly done, and the building of the new school was begun. For the next several months, Dr. Jeff continued to send funds for the building of the school. Many of these funds came from Rotarians in the US and some came from Rotary International. A large part of the funds came directly from Jeff. The only thing left to do for the new school, when the funds finally ran out, was to put the roof onto the building. Jeffrey dug into his personal savings and sent the funds to the Rotarians so that the roof could be placed and the school opened for serving these students.

Besides actually doing medical treatments, Dr. JT did a good amount of health education for the islanders. On one occasion, when Jeff had taken along four nurses to assist in training, he was assigned facilities in an older school building. The group was to teach first aid, care of the elderly and the newborn, sexually transmitted diseases, hypertension, diabetes, and CPR and basic life support. The word was put out by the local Rotarians that Dr. Truzzell and his nursing team would be there on the island to train locals in these six fields of health care. Ladies walked for miles from all over the island to come to this

seminar. Dr. Jeff had planned for 35 ladies to be present. 95 ladies showed up for the training. Since the training was to be for three days, there was nowhere to house these "want to be" health providers. Jeff decided that they could not be turned away from their chosen studies.

Jeff and his team quickly discovered that their students did not demand special living facilities. They were happy just sleeping on the floor. On a couple of days, meals were brought to the entire group. These meals were provided by the Rotarians and their wives. When the meals were not provided, the students gathered vegetables from the surrounding area and cooked for themselves. It was very impressive how these islanders could provide for themselves. After their training was completed, these ladies returned to their home communities where they applied their recently acquired health knowledge. Many of them worked in make-shift nursing homes. Some actually found employment at local health clinics. Hospitals were found in only a limited number of towns throughout the island. Some of the ladies traveled to these towns and secured employment there.

After Jeffrey and his health training team finished with the organized school for the 95 students, they took their teachings to local schools where the curriculum was somewhat changed. Before they had traveled to the island, the Minister of Health had called Dr. JT and given him some specific instructions. The minister said that the study of sexually transmitted diseases should be directed to the people with whom they were having the most problems. He told Jeff that the nine through eleven-year-olds were the ones who were suffering the most from these types of diseases. When Jeffrey passed this along to his nurse team, they were all taken back. They would have to design their training so it would be understood by these youngsters. What a task! This was quite different than in the United States.

The nurses did a fine job of conforming to their task of teaching to young students. One of the things that they did was to bring along assorted small rubber bugs. The nurses would throw them up into the air and see which students could collect the most. After the collection and counting was done, the students were told that these rubber bugs were not something to be proud of. They represented the students catching an unknown type of bug that was transmitted sexually.

Their next teaching technique was to choose four different students. These students would stand at the front of the class. On their backs were pinned at random, face down, a fictitious disease assigned to each student. The signs were "PREGNANT," "SYPHILIS," "GONORRHEA," and "NOTHING." Each student in the class was to come up, shake hands with one of the students with the labels, and get in line behind them. No one knew what the person had who they stood behind. After all students had chosen and were in place, the signs were revealed. Those standing behind the student with PREGNANCY were required by their teachers to carry a water-filled balloon around with them all day. This was to signify the responsibility of caring for a newborn. The ones behind SYPHILIS had to go sit in the corner of the classroom and not be included in any play or even partake of any noon meals. They had contracted a disease that completely removed them from normal society. Those with GONORRHEA had to undergo several doses of nasty tasting syrup, which symbolized their having to take medicine to clear up their disease. Obviously, the students that were behind the person with NOTHING written on her back, did not have to suffer any punishment. They simply went about their normal day. This method of teaching made a large impact on the students. The biggest comment was, "If I had known she had this disease, I would not have gotten in her line." This was exactly the point. Most of the time you don't know who does and who does not have the several complications of casual sexual activities.

On one occasion a student fell off the monkey bars and broke his arm. The students, who had just completed their studies in first aid, immediately calmed the boy. They took two sticks and placed them on either side of the boy's arm. They then wrapped the arm, along with the splint sticks, in newspaper and wrapped the entire arm in gauze. When Dr. JT examined the lad's break, he found that it had been cared for quite well. All of the students were commended for their quick actions and their recently acquired knowledge of health factors, some of which might one day save someone's life.

Chapter 7

Once Jeff returned to his regular practice after spending two weeks in the Caribbean, he realized that he had really "caught the bug." That is the bug of feeling that you must continue doing all possible for the service of people less fortunate. He also realized that there was no way for him to discuss this with anyone who hadn't caught this bug. It is like a rite of passage. You must look into the eyes of those thankful patients who, without your assistance, would have had none. There are many who don't understand the pleasure and self-contentment of serving needy people and expecting nothing in return. A simple smile and perhaps a thank you is all that one can expect. That smile is worth more than all the world's riches, but no one will recognize this until they, also, have caught that bug. It is a warm and satisfying feeling of self-worth and achievement.

Now that Jeffrey was back, he had time to contemplate and plan for his next medical mission adventure. He wanted the next service project to be even more challenging than the last. Where could he go? What could he do? Who needed his services the most? All these questions must be considered before his next plans were made.

He enjoyed this planning because it was much like his drawings and planning of his younger years. Now he was actually putting his plans into action. His present plans had to be seriously considered because he knew that it would take a reasonable amount of time for him to get all his equipment and supplies together. Different trips called for different planning, which always kept his work interesting and fun for him. Often he found that there were medical supply companies who would donate some medications and other supplies, such as gauze and bandages. It seemed that there were many people and businesses that wanted to donate material and be a part of Dr. Jeff's worldwide service projects.

After serious consideration, Jeffrey decided that he wanted to direct his next medical mission to Haiti. He thoroughly studied the island and the two nations that occupied it, Haiti and The

Dominican Republic. The Dominican Republic had prosperously taken advantage of the opportunities that came their way. Haiti, on the other hand, had long been under the control of a corrupt, self-centered government and leadership, which cared little to nothing about the welfare of their citizens and residents. This sad fact was only partially understood by Dr. JT. His research of that nation had only partially exposed their shortcomings and criminal activities. Dr. Jeff did learn that quite a few religious denominations had sent representatives to Haiti to assist in their extensive and diverse needs.

These representatives were there with the idea of building churches and temples, clothing the naked, feeding the hungry, and housing the homeless. These were all great goals for which they should reach, however, most of their efforts were shattered by the massive number of undesirables and criminals who had a death grip on the Haitian people. A criminal factor, similar to the Mafia of the USA, would demand tariffs for all relief supplies that came into the country through the airport or the seaport. They also had the power to decide what should be done for the people and what should be left out. They would limit food distributions to the hungry. They felt that hungry people would more readily be submissive to them and the demands of the illegal groups.

During the earthquake that occurred in Haiti a few years before, the federal prison was severely damaged. Thousands of convicted murderers, thieves, rapists, and other undesirables simply walked out of the facility. They were never recaptured. Because of the lack of electricity and therefore the lack of any lighting, when the sun would go down the criminals would come out and take advantage of the other residents. There was no real form of law enforcement. Everyone had to fend for themselves.

All these considerations went into assisting Dr. Jeff in making his decision to travel to Haiti. His plans were admirable; however, he would be faced with a very difficult task. He categorized his desired accomplishments. First, he would see that electrical power would be established through solar power. This would provide for basic lighting. This lighting would reduce the crime rate and make a safer life for many people. Second, he planned to purchase some land and set up community gardens so that the people could provide for themselves. The third thing that he wanted to do was to establish small medical clinics. In these clinics, he would begin to provide medical care. He could not say that he could provide for all the needy for everyone there was needy. No one had any money, even for the basics of life such as clothes, food, and medicine.

Dr. Jeffrey's largest concern was that he was required to try to not offend the "outlaws." He did not want to get them working against him. He had to convince them that what he was doing was not going to conflict with their plans, although he believed that if his plans succeeded their power over the people would be eliminated. Jeff was quite good at meeting with and resolving problems with many different levels of leadership, be they corrupt or not. He had to figure out a plan where he could present his ideas to the local Mafioso group of thugs.

No one in Haiti knew of Dr. Jeff's profession. He liked it that way. He just represented himself as a concerned American who wanted to help relieve the suffering of the people. He went to the leaders of the gangs and offered them money to allow him passage through customs. He also secured their permission to install solar electricity and to build small clinics and housing. Dr. JT had to first give the mob leaders a solar system for their use. There was no way to guarantee that these thugs would not turn on him and take away everything that he had brought to Haiti. That was just a gamble that he would have to take.

After Dr. Truzzell traveled to Haiti on several occasions, he made his final arrangements for working on small cottage housing which would be equipped with solar electricity. There was plenty of space for him to work and build these houses. Almost everything had been damaged or destroyed during the last earthquake. The people were extremely helpful and worked closely with

Jeff in building living facilities for themselves. Wood and tin sheets had to be collected for the roof and walls of the huts. Concrete was mixed on the ground and poured into 10' X 10' foundations for the flooring. Simple wiring was strung in the cottages to provide for a single light and a small fan.

These facilities might seem small, but they were much larger and better than any hut in which they were accustomed to living. Small community areas were set up and equipped with solar systems for the purposes of cooking, social activities, charging cell phones, and providing a charging station for any other type of electronic device. Although these people were extremely poor, they all seemed to have cell phones, and many had laptop computers. These items were readily available on the black market.

When the building of these small living facilities had begun and was progressing favorably, attention was changed to clearing small plots of land in which they could grow vegetables. Several lots of about one-half acre each were cleared of rocks and stone debris.

These lots were spotted in various locations so they would be of close access to all residents. After the lots were cleared, a tall chain link fence was erected around each. Simple plowing and land preparation readied the fields for planting. Jeffrey had brought over several bags of varied seeds, including corn, wheat, lettuce, cabbage, turnips, and a variety of other easy to grow vegetables. Some of the residents were more experienced in farming and agriculture than were others. They were chosen to till the fields and to plant the various seeds. Another group was chosen to be watchmen and to protect the gardens and keep out those who did not have permission to be there.

At the suggestion of some of the locals, Jeff decided to plant different seeds in different food plots. When mature, all the products could be shared among the workers. Corn and wheat

n

eeded more room, so they had to be planted in separate lots. Various other vegetables could be combined in other lots around the community.

The seeds were watered and soon the plants begin to appear. This was of great pride to the residents and they took much pleasure in keeping the food plots in good shape and keeping the weeds out. They knew that this was going to be their food and they would fight for it if necessary.

The small homes were ample for the needs of the local people. They took much pride in keeping their hut clean and properly managed.

The solar powered electricity was working out great. In several locations, one large solar system was installed to provide electricity to six individual homes. This sharing of power served as an ideal way to bring residents together and establish special bonding.

All seemed to be going extremely well. Aid was provided by some of the religious groups that had come to the island. They saw that more was being accomplished by Jeff's group than by theirs. They were happy to pitch in and help serve the needy people, in whatever way that was needed. Often Jeffrey's group would give aid to the church groups, especially when they needed supplies that were left over from Jeff's building projects.

Next Dr. JT felt ready to build a small clinic where he could provide much needed medical care. It was fairly easy to secure a location and build the clinic. What was difficult was Jeff telling the group that he would be the doctor of the clinic. He decided to first secure a few ladies that wanted to be trained in the basics of health care. These ladies would be called "nurses." Everyone liked having a title, which made them feel important. The nurses were trained to do bandages, splints, and other minor medical procedures. They were taught to use instruments to take blood pressures and to use devices to determine blood sugar levels. Some of them became so advanced that they could make primary diagnoses. All these things would help save precious time that Dr. JT needed for delivering professional medical care. Soon the residents realized that Jeffrey was a real doctor. They had seen him sweat and help with the labors of building houses and clearing garden plots. Now they could see him provide a service that no one else could do. Previously, no one could afford to go to a real doctor. "Medical advisors" and "Voodoo healers" were present, but there was no trained medical doctor to be had. There were many who required good medical care. Now they were blessed with the services of one who was trained to provide their health needs and properly care for them.

Dr. JT knew that there was nothing that these people could do to repay him for his efforts. He explained to them that his only need and concern was for them to join together and protect that which had been given to them. Their houses and their food plots were extremely vital to their wellbeing. Only by standing together could they retain that which they now had. Dr. Jeff was now somewhat at ease, knowing that his new friends and neighbors would always be there to guard and protect him and all that he had done for them.

Dr. Truzzell found himself traveling to Haiti about every two weeks. He would work at home, in his personal practice, for two weeks and then spend two weeks in Haiti. Luckily Jeffrey had associates in his home practice, which made it possible for him to take off to work on his international mission work. He was also blessed by having a staff set up in Haiti at his office there. They were able to set up his schedule for when he was there and see to his patients needing minor medical care while he was away. One of Jeff's major functions, when he was on the Island, was the inoculation of children to prevent major communicable diseases. He also set up special clinical time for family planning. This clinic included providing pregnancy tests and helping the young women learn about preventing unwanted pregnancies. The family planning clinic also allowed for him to diagnose sexually transmitted diseases which was a major medical problem for these people.

Within a couple of years, Dr. JT found that he had many volunteer doctors who wanted to serve in his Haitian health clinics, and they were able to staff his island offices almost constantly. This made it feasible for Jeffrey to spend more of his time planning for other international medical mission work.

Where would he go now and what would he do? By this time, Dr. Jeff was well known by many doctors, worldwide. Doctors without borders, HOPE, the World Health Organization, along with others knew that Dr. JT was someone that they could count on. He asked for their guidance on which areas could most benefit from his services. Although India never had much attraction for him, Jeff felt that this would probably be the next area of his projects' attention. India had many inhabitants requiring more medical attention than they were receiving. He asked himself, "How could he be of the most service to the people of India?" This would take quite a bit of contemplations and planning. This was one of JT's strongest suits and he was ready and willing to take on this mission.

Chapter 8

Jeff told the several worldwide medical service groups that he was thinking of going to India for setting up needed medical care there. Several of his medical cohorts suggested that, because of his superior leadership qualities, as well as special abilities to render the needed medical care, he should spend his time setting up schools for training medical personnel and assistants. In India, there were many intelligent and capable people that sincerely wanted to be trained to be in the medical field. These people had no ready cash that would allow for them to travel to areas where medical training was available. They would be more than happy to study medicine if it were offered, at a nominal fee, within their area.

Dr. Jeffrey, along with several other medical personnel, traveled to India to meet with doctors there who were interested in establishing a medical school and health training facilities. The

Indian medical personnel believed that several satellite medical facilities should be established in different areas of the country. There should be a central, larger, main health facility established in a major centralized city. Using this plan, more people would be able to be trained, both for medicine and for health assisting. India is such a large country, with so very many people, that they needed many health personnel in various areas of their country. A training program, such as this plan of Dr. Jeff's, would be ideal for serving the most possible patients in the largest amount of area in India.

This time Dr. Truzzell had bitten off an extra-large amount of responsibility. He not only had to deal with the many patients, he also had to deal with the local officials, all of whom were certain that their way of accomplishing Jeff's goals was the best. Disagreements arose and soon it was seen that it was much easier to deal with smaller groups of people. Haiti seemed a breeze when compared to the problems in India. In India, it was like establishing 100 different Haitian villages. Not only were ideas very different in

India, the people's cultures and religious beliefs were as varied as night and day. One group was Hindu and another Muslim. One was Christian and another Buddhist. Almost no one could agree with another on any of the major issues at hand. The only thing that they really believed was that their individual thoughts, feelings and opinions were the correct ones, and everyone else should believe the way that they did.

Then there was the cast society, like a class designation, where some people thought that they were better than others. No one of a particular cast would

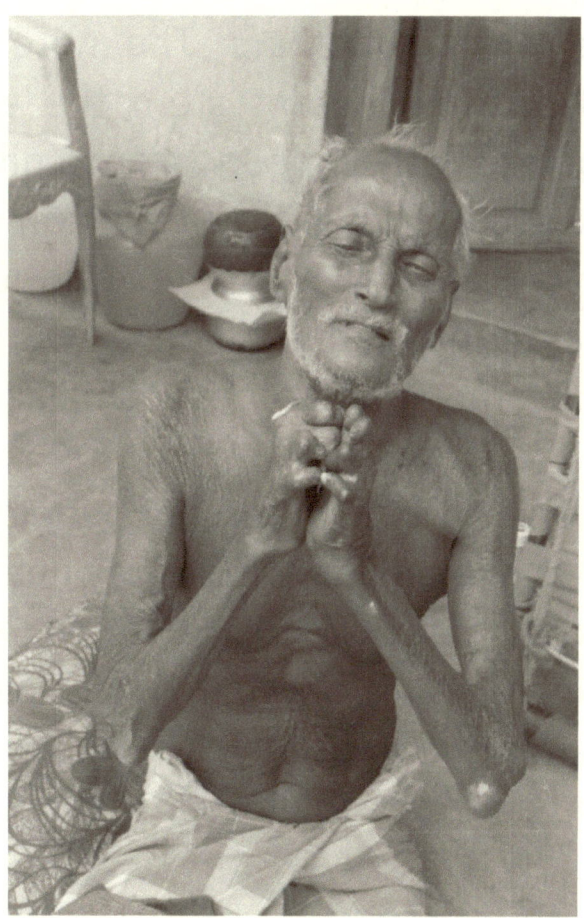

associate with anyone of a different cast. The great need for medical attention was obvious by looking at the sickly and deformed people who lined the streets. If one group felt better than another, little to no aid could be offered to those who were not of their cast. They all wanted to remain in their own cast and with their local residents.

Working with the leaders was almost as bad. Many of them placed themselves above the social ranking of others. The more one was involved in their cast system, the less they would cooperate with someone from a different cast. Most doctors had little interaction with citizens of lower casts. Most of the attention, especially in the remote and rural areas, was given to people among the same, or similar casts.

This division of casts of people caused a serious dilemma for Dr. Jeffrey and his fellow workers. He could not just come in and expect to eliminate the cast system, which had been in place for hundreds of years. His only solution would be to set up different schools and training facilities in different areas, so that they might be capable of treating people of their own social status. None of this made any sense to Jeff for his only concern was to serve all the people with proper medical attention. If the cast system was how medicine must be practiced, then so be it. Although this division of people would cause Jeff's medical clinics and training facilities to be a repetition of each other, he must respect the local wishes of the people. Perhaps someday they would see that they could accomplish more if they would all work together and forget about the different levels of casts of individuals.

Dr. Jeff spent most of his time with planning and office work, and little actual medical treatment. He interviewed and hired several nurses and health assistants to work in the various clinics. Jeffrey first established small clinics in remote communities where there were no doctors. After the medical facilities were established, he set up centralized schools where the health professionals could come and study the intricate parts of practicing medicine. These medical schools were located about 200 miles from each other. This allowed students to travel to and from the schools. The classes were set up on a two-week on and two-week off cycle. This schedule went on until the students were prepared to delve deeper into the science of actually practicing medicine. By the third year of study, if a student had made it that far, the curriculum was changed to three months on and one month off. During the off months the students were to return to their villages where they would participate in delivering basic medical care.

This system was very effective and soon there were many health professions, including surgeons and general physicians, who were trained and ready to be assigned back into their home communities. This worked out to be an ideal way to provide medical personnel for all areas of this vast country. Some of the students that had no means of repaying any school dept were placed for a two-year intern period in rural, less desirable areas of the country to pay off their debts. This provided medical care for people in remote areas, as well as providing a specialized type of medical training for the doctors.

Rural medicine provided a completely different type of medical training. Often there were tiger maulings, elephant trampling, monkey bites, and other sorts of broken bones and lacerations. A physician never had a dull day when practicing in the country. Many of the patients required treatment for worms, dysentery, typhoid fever, and other common ailments for that region. Once a woman who had just delivered a baby was brought in by her husband. She was suffering from a retained placenta. There were very few medical supplies. The physician preformed a dilation and curettage, sutured the patient up with dental sutures, labeled where each stitch went, and gave her a partial transfusion of blood from her husband. She was then fed extensive amounts of coconut water. Within five days the patient was well enough to be taken home.

Because of the foresight, many students were trained to care for the health needs of the residents in their home areas. Many patients were blessed with the presence of medical treatments. The extensive outreach of Dr. Truzzell's medical schools in India, along with the large number of students wanting to be trained in medical sciences, provided for a nationwide access to health treatments. This project was unquestionably the most effective disbursement of medical services undertaken by Dr. Jeff anywhere in the world.

JT's major goal was now to improve the health facilities of the various locations which he had established. Many areas were suffering from their inability to provide proper sterilization. There were autoclaves in some areas, however, it took electricity to operate these devices. Electricity, for the most part, was only produced by the use of generators. It took expensive fuel to operate the generators, if the fuel was even available. Diseases could spread and epidemics could break out simply because the original infection was not controlled with sterilization. AIDS, Ebola, and diseases of the like were often spread because there was not proper cleanliness and sterilization at the initial treatment sites.

Chapter 9

Dr. Jeffrey had been well trained in the use of solar devices for producing electricity. He had even designed a special battery backup system for use where there was no grid electricity. He went on to secure a US patent on the solar device, not so that no one else could use it but so that the device would be properly used. He was now putting his efforts into improving the recently patented solar system. The largest problem that he faced was that there were few manufacturers who had ever worked with such a device. Grid tied electric solar systems were commonly used, however there were few, or no, battery backed units.

After locating the proper equipment and designing a systematic arrangement for its connections, he was faced with the problem of finding batteries that could charge quickly and last a long time between replacements. He went through many types of these "deep cycle" batteries, both lead and AGM (glass mat). None of these batteries were meeting his needs and expectations. Finally, Jeff discovered manufacturers that were producing Lithium based batteries. Although the lithium was more difficult to come by, the batteries lasted for up to 25 years. This was ideal for use with solar systems in remote locations, along with locations that did not have the financial means to keep replacing the batteries.

When taken to the Army Corps of Engineers, where they were tested, demonstrated, and accepted, the lithium batteries were quickly adopted for immediate installation. There was much interest among the military branches as to how these devices could also be used in remote areas and war zones which had little to no electricity. The military would no longer have to depend on gas guzzling generators to produce their electricity. These solar systems could be dropped into any area and immediately be put to work. Lighting, the use of computers, and many other functions could be performed with little effort and no noise, either during the daytime or at night. The military appreciated this new technology that provided solar systems equipped with the specialized batteries. This, however, was not the purpose for which Jeff had designed the systems. It was good that they could be used in this manner, however, in his mind the provision of health needs was foremost.

The Corps of Engineers suggested that JT take the solar devices to FEMA, where they could be used in areas of disasters and the loss of grid electricity. There were many such areas for FEMA. They could be used after hurricanes, in areas of large fires, earthquakes, and floods. As is most always the case with federal agencies, FEMA kept running into difficulties. Hurricanes came and went. Floods and fires occurred. All with no action on the part of FEMA to provide solar systems for their relief efforts. The delays in providing these solar units had to do with obtaining approval by the top echelon of the group. It was now proven that Jeff's solar devices could be used for health care, military instillations, disaster relief, and even for the reduction of electrical use for normal homes and offices. What were they waiting for? The best things are often the last to be accepted.

Dr. Jeff would not wait for anyone to proceed with the use of his solar systems in health departments. They could run autoclaves, lights, fans, air conditioners, and stoves, basically any device requiring electricity. JT began securing financial aid for purchasing these systems. He arranged for his teams of experts to travel to different areas to assist in installing the first of these devices. Before the year was out, Jeff had twelve health facilities operating on his solar systems. There were clinics in Haiti, Africa, India and in South America. Soon the device's use spread to other areas. The only thing that was slowing the installations down was the fact that several large electric companies wanted to get their hands into the action. They didn't want to lose any of their profits by sharing with any outsider. No matter what the laudable function of the solar system was to be, the big businesses wanted to quell the expansion so that they might be included in the profits, even though they had nothing to do with its instillation or expansion.

Solar power was just one of the alternative options. There also were hydrodynamics, geothermal, nuclear reactors, and wind turbines. All of these would be much better for the future survival of the earth than burning fossil fuels. The mining of fossil fuels, and the production of electricity from burning them, had the largest political lobby of any company in the US. How could anyone expect to change legislation with that kind of money being spent to maintain the status quo? Dr. Jeff knew more about solar power than of any of the other power alternatives. He also knew about providing health care. A healthy environment, along with the provision of medical care, could easily go hand-in-hand with solar powered electrical production. Dr. Jeffrey knew how to argue his points about providing health care. He knew nothing of the political hoodwinking or dealing with lobbyist and the large finance business firms. Although he had received several honorary doctorate degrees, many international service awards, and been nominated for the Nobel Prize for Medicine, JT found himself at a dead end. Good intentions were no match for under the table financial dealings.

Sadness now filled his heart for he knew that those who strove for fortune and fame would certainly win out over those whose intentions were simply to do good for the needy. The business world was not a place for the meek at heart. It seemed like only the financially strong would survive. As a trickle of a tear ran down his cheek, however, he was encouraged by remembering all the people that he had served. Although he had grown out of his league in the world of finance, Jeff still knew that there were many left in his path that sincerely appreciated and prospered from all that he had done. His time had now come to retreat to his simple, small practice of family medicine. He would spend his remaining days reflecting on all his laudable achievements and dedication to the service of others. Perhaps he would write some stories about his experiences. Perhaps he would record all his efforts in a journal that could someday be shared with his grandchildren.

Jeff had now run the gambit from being a wild-eyed dreamer of fantasies that seemed to be beyond his expectations of completion, to a well known and respected physician with many completed projects that would, for a long time to come, serve the many needy people around the world.

Now that Jeffrey had settled down from his constant running from place to place, building health clinics, medical schools, and providing services to the less fortunate, he was being called upon to present lectures and write papers for many prestigious health organizations. On  several occasions, he was asked to be the keynote speaker for a conference or convention. This activity brought much delight to JT. He could remember the times when he was ridiculed by his classmates for coming up with projects that they could not understand. Now, having broken through the barrier of understanding and acceptance by his colleagues, he was delighted and proud to stand before august groups of learned people and present his ideas. Now his ideas didn't seem so strange.

A copy of his first, and most self satisfying, speech, was kept in a safe place. This speech was given by him at the convention of one of the largest service organizations in the world. This was his keynote speech.

"I have stood on the pinnacle of the highest mountain and I have crawled through the lowest valley. I have consorted with kings and I have gathered morsels with the lowest of mankind. I have reveled with politicians and I have suffered with those that the political system represses. I am as great as any person on earth and yet I am no better than anyone else. I am a creature of God and within me dwells the Spirit that was placed there by my Creator.

"I have set my ship afloat to drift with the ebb and flow of the tides of the sea of life. At times the currents were favorable and I was able to make great progress, however, there were times the currents were unfavorable and directed me to regress. No matter the direction, I always breathed in the fresh air of the breezes of the sea and I gave thanks for the blessings that had been bestowed upon me. When the winds were in my favor, I was able to unfurl the sails of my ship and accomplish great things. When the tempests would come, I would quickly strike the main and furl the jib until conditions became favorable again.

"I have traveled on my journey with the clear understanding that what I gave to my fellow man, I also gave to myself. There were stumbling blocks along the way which refused to be loved but I accepted them as learning tools for myself. Rather than turning back and learning to hate, I chose to plunge forward and learn to love, even deeper and better than before. Often it is through the sincere attempt to understand others that one learns to understand oneself.

"It is only through meditation and self understanding that one can become all that one can be. The temple of God lies within each and every human. Only through self realization can one realize what and who he really is. Once this is understood, there is a pressing desire to give of oneself to others through assistance of whatever is needed. The help given is never for physical rewards, for a truly awakened soul is far above that. The true reward is in seeing a fellow man rise to new heights for himself, spiritually and physically. As was stated by the Great Teacher, 'freely you have received therefore freely give.'

"I personally find embarrassment in the receiving of awards and honors for it is not to this end that I have served. My only joy in receiving these human gestures is the hope that they may encourage others to seek a way to serve their fellow man. It is only with the open hand of sharing that one is truly allowed to receive. It is only through a sincere desire to understand that one may be understood. Through love, the greatest of virtues, all things are possible. If one seeks true honor and respect from oneself, his peers, and his God, he must direct his actions, with his sincerest love, toward his fellow man."

www.ingramcontent.com/pod-product-compliance
Lightning Source LLC
Chambersburg PA
CBHW051308250626
47155CB00009B/3488